For my parents, with love and thanks. MZ

For Hollie Rose, with love. AW

Rita wants a Fairy Godmother published by Graffeg in 2022.
Copyright © Graffeg Limited 2022.

ISBN 9781802580440

First published by An tSnáthaid Mhór Teoranta, 2017.

Text © Máire Zepf, illustrations © Andrew Whitson, design
and production Graffeg Limited. This publication and
content is protected by copyright © 2022.

Máire Zepf and Andrew Whitson are hereby identified as
the authors of this work in accordance with section 77 of the
Copyrights, Designs and Patents Act 1988.

A CIP Catalogue record for this book is available from the
British Library.

Mae Rita Eisiau Tylwythen Deg (Welsh edition)
ISBN 9781802580457
Rita agus an tSióg Mhaith (Irish edition) ISBN 9781912929184

The publisher acknowledges the financial support of the
Books Council of Wales. www.gwales.com.

Teaching Resources
www.graffeg.com/pages/teachers-resources

1 2 3 4 5 6 7 8 9

This book belongs to

_____

_____

_____

_____

GRAFFEG

Rita

wants a Fairy Godmother

By Máire Zepf

Illustrated by Mr Ando

This is

Rita.

Rita is still not dressed.

Rita wants a fairy godmother.

A fairy godmother would only have to twirl her wand –

swoosh!

– and she would
be dressed.

Her mum would never tell her to hurry up again.

And she wouldn't
need to dress herself
anymore.

She would have the
most beautiful clothes
in the world,

for every occasion.

13

Hopefully, her fairy godmother wouldn't make her *too* fancy.

14

Because that could be really embarrassing.

15

What if she gave her the wrong shoes to wear?

Or even the wrong clothes?

18

What if she didn't know
when to stop?

That would be terrible.

Or what if she thought Rita
should just look pretty

and never get messy

22

A fairy godmother could ruin everything.

And where would it end?

No, Rita has changed her mind.

She doesn't want a fairy godmother after all.

swoosh!

Rita will dress herself.